Undersea Volcanoes

Written by Inbali Iserles

The roasting sea

Picture a volcano. You probably thought of an exploding peak, poking out of a tropical land. Right?

But did you know that most volcanoes are hidden beneath the waves at the bottom of the sea?

Contents

Unit 6

Core: Undersea Volcanoes 6

Challenge: Poles Apart 22

Unit 7

Core: Investigate Green Power 38

Challenge: The Light Thief 54

The term 'volcano' comes from 'Vulcan', the Roman god of fire. Vulcan was known for controlling the fire of volcanoes and deserts, and the flames needed for crafting metal.

How are volcanoes formed?

Our planet's surface is like a giant puzzle. Its crust – the shallow, hard outer layer – is split into pieces called tectonic plates.

These plates are constantly shifting. Over time, some plates grow closer, while some drift apart. Those shifts form volcanoes, which are openings in the crust.

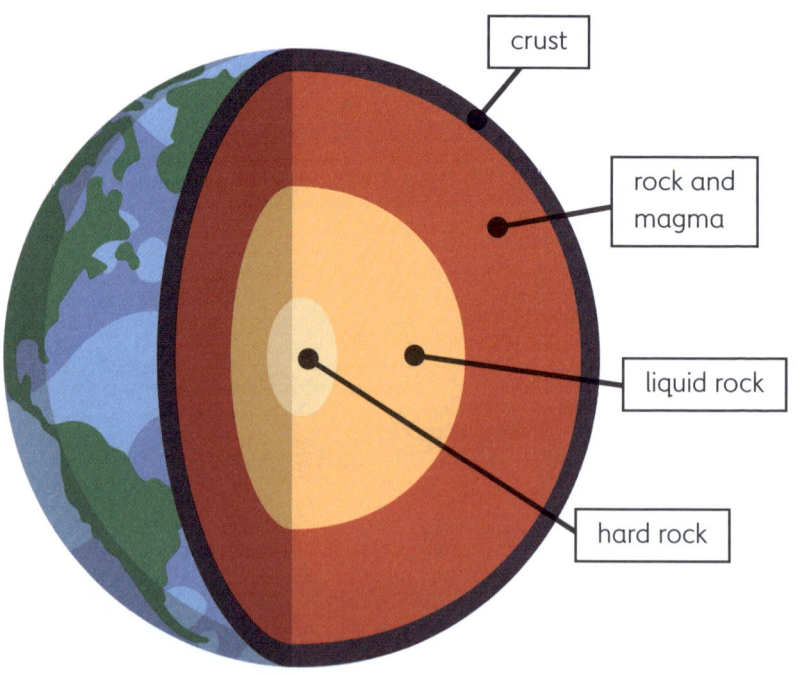

When plates move closer together, they collide and some plates slide below. These plates sink, then heat up and melt to form magma.

When plates pull apart, the crust thins and makes a pathway. Hot magma beneath the plates rises and flows up this pathway.

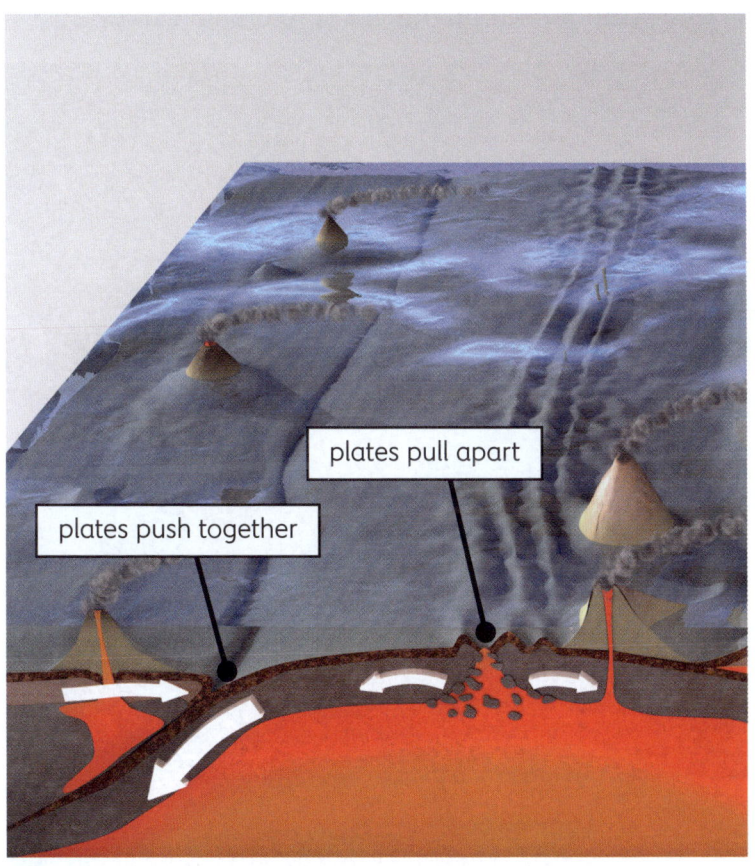

Why do volcanoes erupt?

Imagine bubbles trapped inside a shaken-up bottle of fizzy drink, with nowhere for them to go. Just like the bubbles in the bottle, gas and magma get trapped inside a volcano. This leads to a massive build-up of force that grows stronger and stronger – until the volcano finally explodes!

The gas and magma get pushed up and burst out through cracks in the volcano. The force of an erupting volcano can send scorching lava, ash and toxic gases flying for miles.

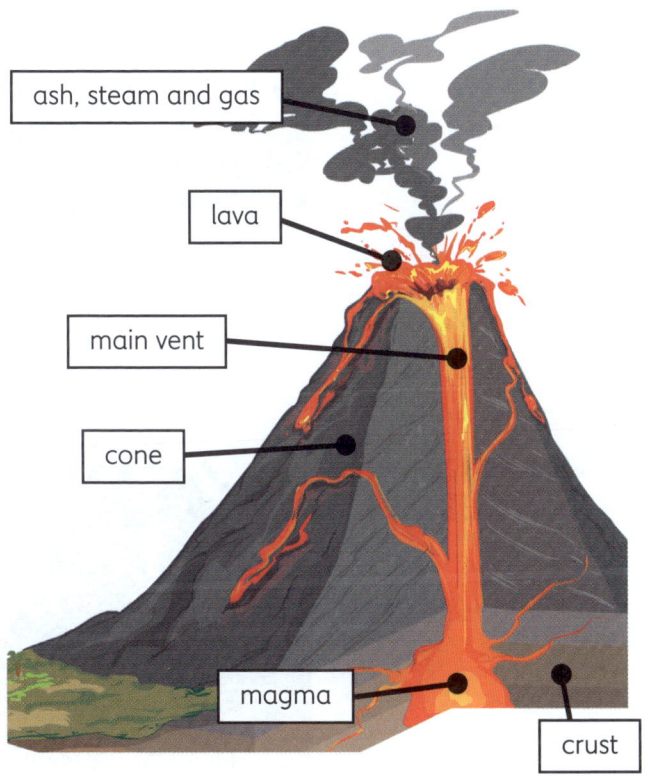

ash, steam and gas

lava

main vent

cone

magma

crust

Once magma is outside a volcano, it's called lava. Lava can reach over 1,250 °C – that's over 10 times hotter than boiling water!

There are over 1,000 active volcanoes across the globe, and they come in many shapes. Two examples are:

Shield volcanoes, which have low, wide domes that look like giant shields lying on the land.

Composite volcanoes, which are steep and cone shaped, and are famed for their destructive force when they erupt.

Volcanoes of the deep

You won't see an underwater volcano from a beach. But when a massive one erupts, it can create colossal waves that crash over the coast.

There could be over 1,000,000 unknown volcanoes lurking below the sea!

An undersea volcano erupts near Tonga.

Hydrothermal vents: hotspots for life

But don't be too frightened – undersea volcanoes help create life!

- When tectonic plates pull apart on the seabed, seawater flows deep into the crust.

- The magma below heats the water and minerals dissolve in it.

- Streams of hot, mineral-rich water shoot up and burst out of holes in the crust, called 'hydrothermal vents'.

- As hot streams mix with cold seawater, the minerals cool and form hard 'chimneys'.

Tiny living things called microbes feed on these minerals. Creatures, like crabs, make their homes near the chimneys, feasting on the microbes.

Who'd have known that such a harsh environment could be a bustling habitat?

Pillow lava: nature's art

When sizzling magma from undersea volcanoes meets cold seawater, it cools quickly. As magma cools, it hardens into shapes known as 'pillows'. These pillows lie in rows on the seabed, forming patterns.

These patterns are important as they are a sign of volcanic activity nearby.

Life without light

Exploring the deepest parts of our seas is a challenge, but scientists know that life thrives even in the dark, cold depths.

Creatures live in cosy holes under volcanic vents. These vents lie deeper than 2.5 kilometres beneath the surface!

There's still so much to find out when it comes to undersea volcanoes. Studying these fascinating habitats can help us unlock the secrets of our planet.

Fossils show that many of the oldest plants and animals lived under the sea, back when life didn't yet exist on land. Was it in the deep, dark heat of underwater volcanoes that life began?

Spotlight on: the Havre volcano

In 2012, a passenger on a plane was flying home from a holiday in Samoa. When the passenger looked out of the window, she spotted something important, by chance! She noticed a large, grey-brown mass floating on the surface of the sea. She took photos and sent them to a volcanologist.

The mass turned out to be giant lumps of volcanic rock, from an erupting underwater volcano! Volcanologists investigated this further and came across the Havre volcano.

Havre volcano

The Havre volcano is one of the biggest undersea volcanoes on the planet. It lies 900 metres beneath the sea's surface, in the Pacific.

With samples from a trip to the volcano, scientists hope to find out exactly what makes an underwater volcano erupt.

Poles Apart

Written by Samantha Montgomerie

Illustrated by Monique Steele

Leo stretched his fingers over the wide expanse of the map.

"We'll be poles apart," he said, grimacing.

He trailed his finger slowly across the map to Canada.

"No, not quite poles apart. Unlike you, I won't be in a snowy home at the end of the globe," Sophia said.

"I know. But it feels so far!" Leo groaned.

Leo looked at the wide mass of Antarctica on the map. On Sunday, he was going to the frozen continent with his dad. His dad's team were collecting data to monitor ice melt.

Going to Antarctica would be amazing! Going weeks without seeing Sophia was not so great.

Sophia wiggled her phone. "Keep me posted when you can," she said. "I'll follow everything!"

A week later, a boat carved a trail through the icy sea. Towering peaks rose to the sky, glowing in their snowy whiteness. They had been at Rothera Point for three days now, and Leo was still totally amazed by the vast wilderness.

"Whales!" he cried.

Blowhole spray ballooned up high as the humpback whales rose like dark shadows. They burst up, breaching high. Then the sea foamed as it gulped the whales back below.

Icebergs floated like sculpted cathedrals.
Leo spotted a little seal on an ice sheet as they drifted by. He hoped a hunting orca wouldn't take it for a snack!

A bellow boomed from elephant seals, clustered on the edge of the water.

"You can hear them burp from here!" grinned Leo's dad.

They may have been remote but they were far from alone!

Back at the base, Leo followed his dad into the lab.

"Our drilling team has fresh samples," his dad said. "They'll show us what's happening below the ice."

The team showed Leo how they were analysing the data from the samples to look at shifts in the ice shelf.

"These graphs show us the changes over time," explained one of the team members.

"Antarctica's ice is vital to maintaining our planet's balance. Glaciers have melted and refrozen over time as our planet has heated and cooled. But the whole planet is now heating up. Greenhouse gases in the sky have a blanket effect, keeping the cold out and the heat in," she added.

That evening, Leo messaged Sophia to tell her everything. As he was so remote, there was a long wait between messages. But that didn't matter.

> **From:** Leo **To:** Soph
> You know how the planet's heating up? One of Dad's team said that the heating seas at the poles melt the ice from below. So the ice breaks off and ends up melting into the sea.

> **From:** Soph **To:** Leo
> Whoa, that's pretty concerning. What's your dad's team studying exactly?

> **From:** Leo **To:** Soph
> They're looking at this place called the Thwaites Glacier. It basically supports the whole West Antarctic Ice Sheet.

From: Leo   **To:** Soph

Most of the glacier sits below sea level, and the bedrock under it slopes down, so the ice flows faster into the sea.

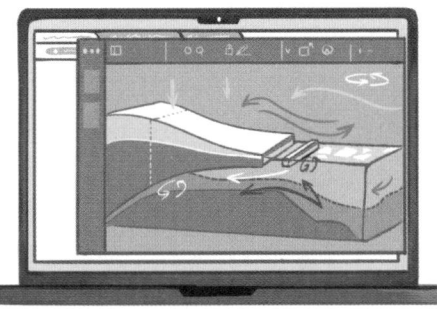

From: Soph   **To:** Leo

So that's what makes the sea levels rise. I remember reading somewhere that coastal places all over the globe are being affected by sea levels rising ... What can we do?

From: Leo   **To:** Soph

Antarctica holds 90% of the planet's ice! (Which is why it's known as the 'frozen continent'.) So, if teams like Dad's can focus on what's happening here, they might work out how we can slow down the rise of sea levels across the globe. And cutting greenhouse gases could delay the ice sheet from collapsing as fast.

Leo strode to the window to look out at the snowy landscape. Finally, a message pinged from Sophia.

From: Soph   **To:** Leo
So basically we need to show people that we're on borrowed time!

From: Leo   **To:** Soph
Exactly! We've all got to step up and follow through.

Leo rested his elbows on the windowsill as he scrolled through the photos on his phone.

Leo woke the next morning and checked for a message from Sophia.

He grinned. It might have taken all night, but she'd got the photos he sent her. And she'd posted them.

Soph_B

We all have a role to protect our planet – from pole to pole.

#ProtectOurHome #GoGreen
♡ 310   💬 54

People from all over the globe had added comments under Sophia's post.

Leo messaged Sophia.

From: Leo   **To:** Soph
You're the best, Soph!

The frozen wilderness glowed in the midnight sun. Leo soaked in the stillness.

It's funny how being far from all you know can help you see what matters the most, he thought.

Gazing at the vast stretch of the sea, he imagined it flowing all over the globe, connecting people from pole to pole.

How the Thwaites Glacier is melting

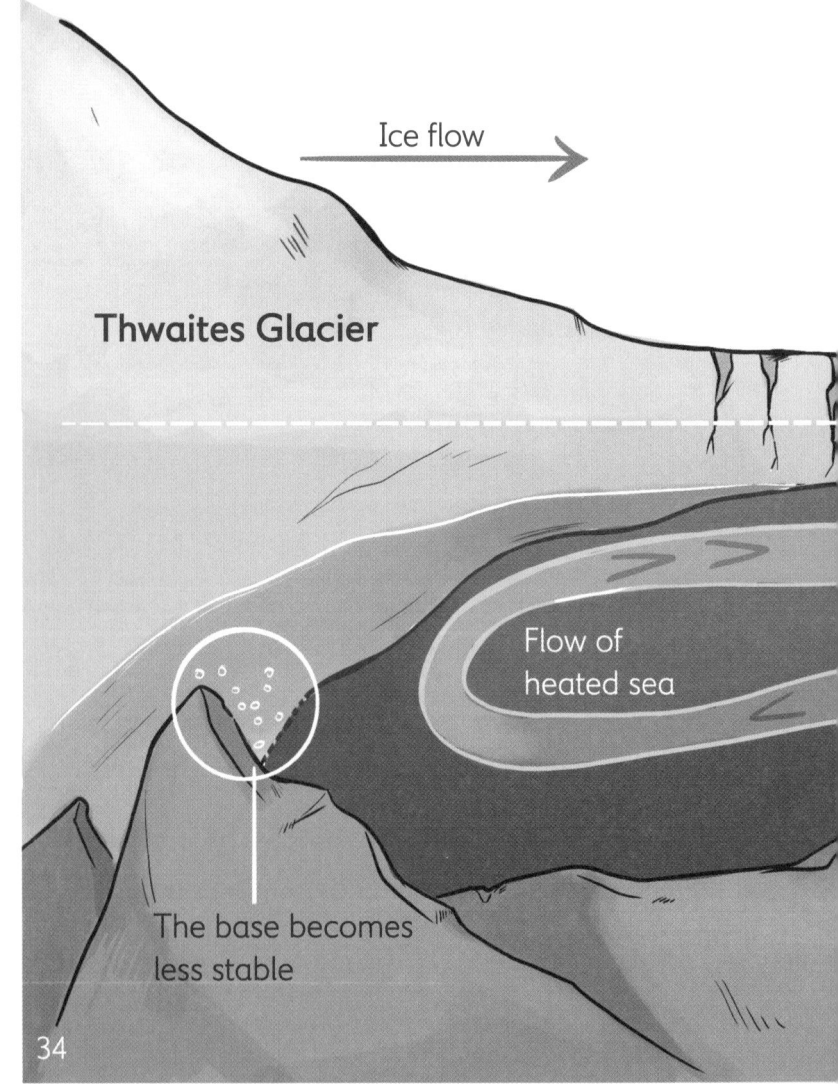

Thwaites
Glacier
Rothera
Point
ANTARCTICA
West Antarctic
Ice Sheet

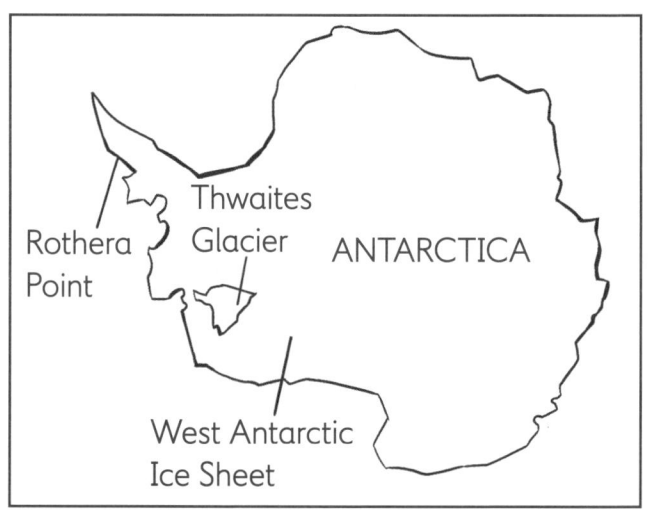

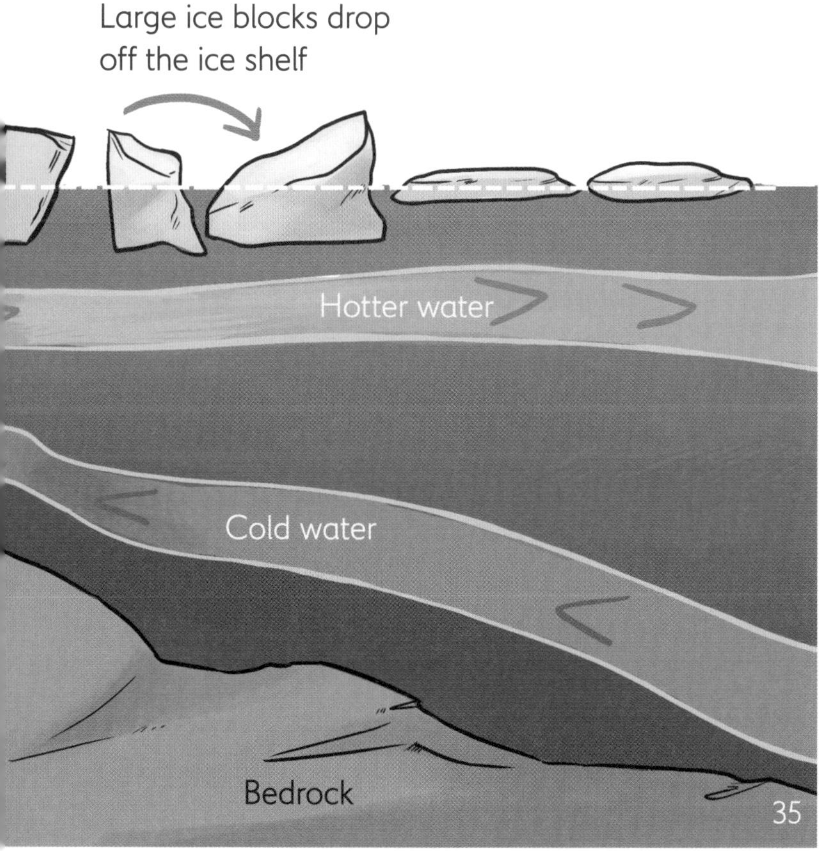

Large ice blocks drop
off the ice shelf
Hotter water
Cold water
Bedrock

Investigate Green Power

Written by Suzy Senior

Energy for living

What do e-scooters, video games and central heating have in common?

They all need power, or energy, to keep them going!

Whether you are:

playing music on your phone

travelling to school on a bus, tram, train or in a car

or relaxing in a cosy home,

energy is a key ingredient we use every day.

Fossil fuels

Until a few years ago, most of our energy came from fossil fuels, which include oil, gas and coal. Power plants burned coal to produce electricity, and people used coal to heat their homes.

Diesel and petrol are refined from crude oil, which is known as petroleum.

So, how were fossil fuels made? Let's go back to prehistoric times: when plants and animals died, they were gradually crushed by layers of rock. Over millions of years, this decomposing matter turned into oil, natural gas and coal.

We mine and drill for these fuels wherever we find them, whether that's below land or under seabeds.

Prehistoric times **Today**

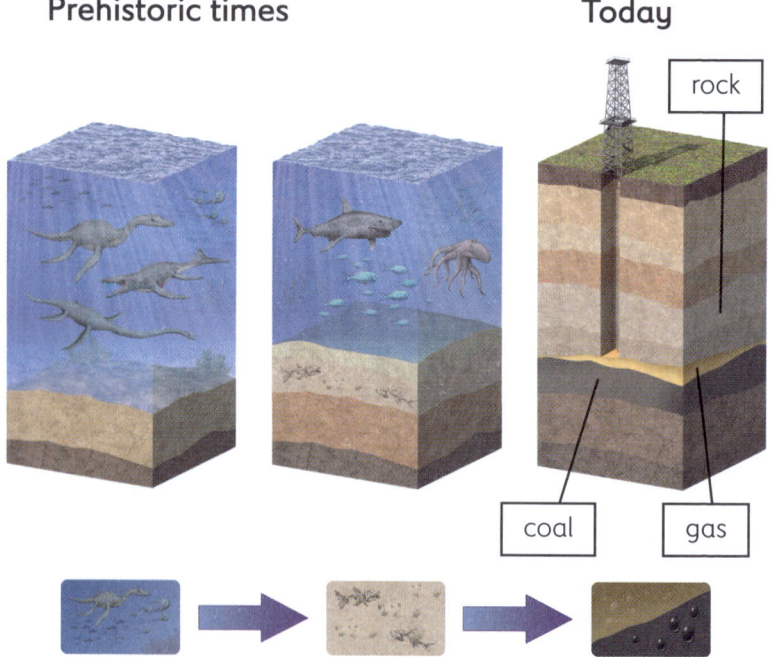

But here's the issue: fossil fuels are non-renewable, meaning they can't be replaced once they are used up. Eventually, they'll run out.

Burning these fuels pollutes our air and produces carbon dioxide, a gas that contributes to climate change. This has negative effects, including extreme temperatures and floods.

Reducing our fossil fuel usage reduces the impact we have on the planet, known as our 'carbon footprint'.

A greener future

Now for some good news! Unlike fossil fuels, green energy is renewable, meaning it won't run out. Since 2023, the UK has been using a greater percentage of renewable energy than fossil fuels. In fact, the last coal-fired power plant in the UK closed in 2024.

Let's investigate some ways to generate renewable electricity. How many do you recognise?

Solar and hydropower

Solar panels are like magic screens that convert sunlight into electricity. You can find them on rooftops, in fields and even on lamp-posts.

Have you ever come across hydropower? This uses tides, waves or dammed rivers to produce electricity. Moving water generates kinetic energy, which spins turbines inside hydroelectric dams to create energy.

dam

turbines

Kinetic energy is energy stored in a moving object.

Wind and geothermal power

Have you ever seen wind turbines in fields or out at sea? They're super important as they catch the wind and turn it into energy.

Wind farms provided most of the UK's renewable energy in 2024.

Some homes in suitably windy places have their own mini-turbines for power.

We can even use our planet's heat to produce renewable energy. Piping water through hot rocks beneath the surface produces steam, which turns turbines and generates electric power.

Iceland's volcanic geology is perfect for geothermal power plants.

Many newer homes in the UK now have individual geothermal pumps to heat their water.

Bioenergy

Did you know that we can burn organic matter, including crops, wood, and even food and animal waste, to create energy? It's called biomass. It can be used to heat buildings or produce electricity.

This furniture business uses its own waste wood as biomass to heat the factory's units. This reduces its carbon footprint, and its energy and waste disposal bills. It's a win-win!

Many cars now run on electricity, but we can process biomass to make renewable eco-fuels, too. Biodiesel is a liquid biofuel made from plant oils, while biogas is produced when plant or animal waste is broken down by micro-organisms.

Sunflowers aren't just pretty: they can feed animals and humans, and can be turned into biofuels!

Nuclear power

We can make electricity with nuclear power, too. When nuclear fuels like uranium and plutonium react, they produce heat. This turns water into steam, which spins turbines in power plants.

Just a tiny bit of nuclear fuel can create huge volumes of electricity without releasing greenhouse gases or polluting the air.

However, nuclear power has downsides. It is non-renewable, so it could run out. Radioactive waste is harmful, too, and must be stored safely for 1000s of years.

So, energy powers our lives, and while fossil fuels have been our go-to for ages, we need to prioritise greener energy. It's important that we keep exploring and finding new ways to protect our planet.

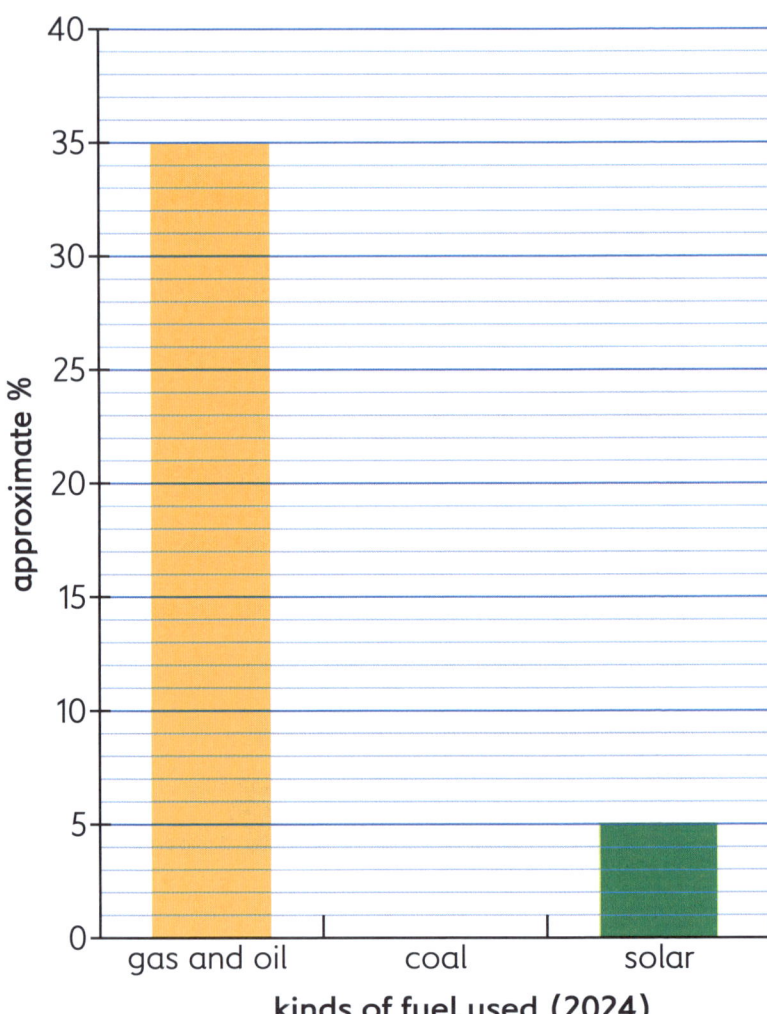

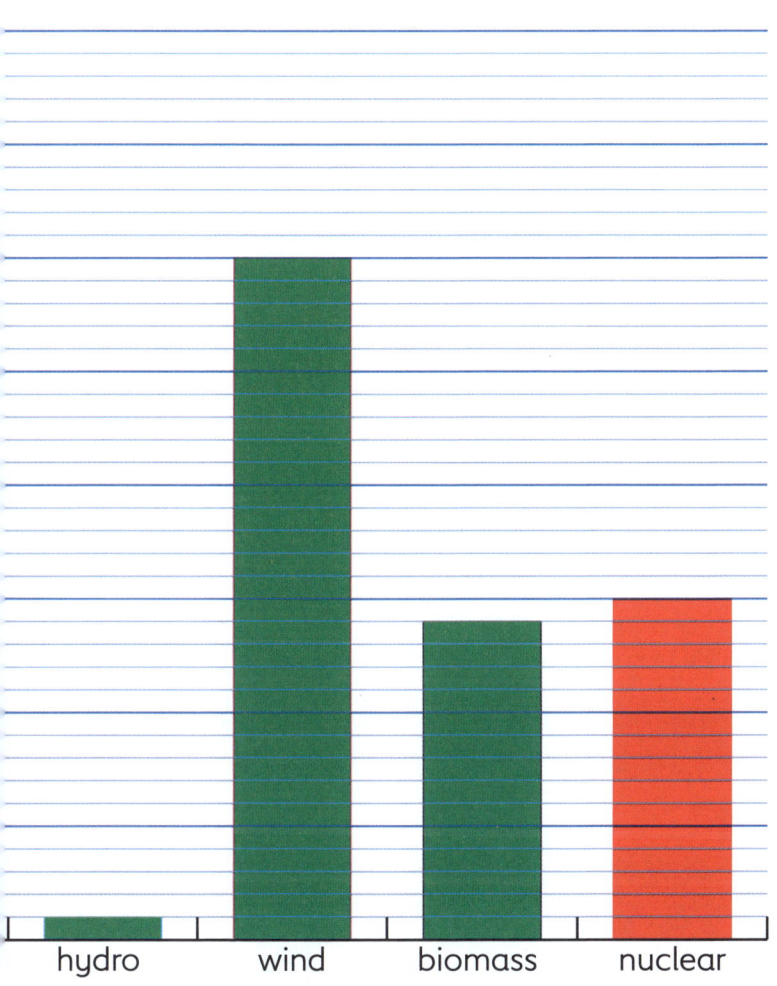

In 2024, renewable energy overtook fossil fuels in the UK. Until then, fossil fuels often supplied most of the UK's electricity.

The Light Thief

Written by Lindsay Galvin

Illustrated by Hannah Drennan

"We've got a customer," said Nico's dad.

Nico had spotted her as soon as she'd come in. She had eaten at his family's new beach taverna for the last few nights. She kept crossing his mind – she was cute.

Nico's mum appeared from the kitchen, frowned and looked at the clock. They should've stopped serving food by now. They needed help in the kitchen but they'd had issues getting staff.

The customer sat at the same table as yesterday, midway down the beach, in the moonlight. Her hair blew in the wind.

Nico handed her a menu. "Hello again," he said. "I'm Nico."

"I know – it says Nico on your badge," she said, pointing at his uniform.

Nico's cheeks burned.

"I'll have a grapefruit juice and fries, please," she added.

Nico was dying to ask her name but went mute.

"I'm Ruby, by the way," she said, grinning.

Later, Nico scooped Ruby some free ice-cream, planning to act cool as he gave it to her. But when he turned back, she was gone. His whole body slumped.

That night, Nico was woken by his dad yelling. He flew out of bed and ran across the poolside next to their apartment and into the taverna.

"Someone has smashed every single light bulb," said his mum, dabbing her eyes.

The next day, they fitted new bulbs.

But the following night, the cords leading to the lights were cut.

"This can't continue. We need security cameras," said Nico's mum.

"Truth is, we can't afford them," said Nico's dad.

Nico's shoulders tensed. For years, his parents had run a little coffee shop in Athens, saving to afford this beach taverna in Crete.
He had no clue why someone would do this.

Later that night, when everyone was asleep, Nico hid in the shadows by the side of the taverna. He knew his parents wouldn't support his plan to catch the vandal red-handed.

The moon was like a shiny jewel over the sea. The beach grew cooler, the sand now damp with dew. Nico's eyelids drooped.

Suddenly, a dark figure scuttled along the beach and up between the tables. Nico fumbled with his phone and started to film.

The figure had a cap on and a tube scarf pulled up to obscure their face. They carried a long tool.

They raced into the taverna, dragged up a stool and climbed on it, reaching up to the security light Nico's parents left on all night.

Nico had planned to stay hidden and film this so he had proof. But he couldn't help himself.

"Hey, stop!" he yelled.

The figure sprang off the stool and flew across the taverna. They dodged between the tables on the sand.

Nico ran after them. The person was shorter than him, but fast, and he had to sprint to keep up. He stopped filming to run faster.

"Hey – why? Why are you doing this?" he cried out as he started to trail behind.

The person stopped suddenly, arms outstretched. Sand sprayed by their feet.

"Get back!" they yelled with such panic that Nico stopped in his tracks. He couldn't believe his ears.

"Ruby? Is that you?" said Nico, panting.

"Don't move. Be quiet. Please," said Ruby. She knelt down, looking at something.

"OK, OK," said Nico. The panic in her voice told him not to argue.

"It's started," said Ruby.

Nico gasped. He could see the sand move! He knelt down next to her.

In the moonlight, the sand was shades of blue and grey. Shadowy patches were scuttling! One was shuffling to Nico.

"Baby ... turtles!" said Nico, reaching out, full of amazement.

"Don't!" snapped Ruby, pulling her tube scarf down. "They are newborn and very fragile."

"They hatch from a nest in the sand and are led to the sea by the moon. But electric lights confuse them," she explained.

Nico sprinted back to the taverna and switched off the security light. The beach fell dark.

Back at the hatching site, the turtles now scuttled down to the sea by the light of the moon. A tiny one struggled, so Ruby smoothed out a flat path for it.

Ruby and Nico gazed at the edge of the water as the last of the turtles swam off.

"The females will come back to this exact beach to lay their own eggs," said Ruby.

"How do you know all this?" said Nico.

"We studied it at school. I want to be a turtle expert one day," said Ruby.

"Why didn't you just tell us that the lights were a problem?" asked Nico.

"I presumed you were like the last owners. I tried explaining to them time and time again, but they didn't value the turtles," she said. "I know it's not an excuse for the damage. I'm truly sorry."

"We'll make sure the light doesn't disturb them in future," said Nico. "And I have an idea of how you can make up for the damage."

The next day, Nico served Ruby her fries and grapefruit juice. But this time she was on her break, and the whole family was very happy with their new kitchen worker.

Life cycle of a sea turtle

Female turtles lay eggs on the beach.

Female turtles return to the same beach.

Newborn turtles hatch from the eggs.

Baby turtles are led to the sea by the moon.

Acknowledgements

The publishers gratefully acknowledge the permission granted to reproduce the copyright material in this book. Every effort has been made to trace copyright holders and to obtain their permission for the use of copyright material. The publishers will gladly receive any information enabling them to rectify any error or omission at the first opportunity.

pp6-7 Justin Kase zsixz/Alamy Stock Photo, p7tr Zwiebackesser/Shutterstock, p9 Christoph Burgstedt/Science Photo Library, p10 Benny Christiansen/Shutterstock, p11 Drp8/Shutterstock, p13 Dana Stephenson/Getty Images, p14 NOAA, p15 David Shale/Nature Picture Library, p16 NOAA, p17 Jose Antonio Peñas/Science Photo Library, pp18-19 Universal Images Group/Getty Images, p38t oatawa/Shutterstock, p38c Leonid Andronov/Shutterstock, p38b Improvisor/Shutterstock, p39 muratart/Shutterstock, p41 VLADJ55/Shutterstock, p42 Designifty/Shutterstock, p43t kabby/Shutterstock, p43bl Autumn Sky Photography/Shutterstock, p43br CrackerClips Stock Media/Shutterstock, p44 Steve Meese/Shutterstock, p45 Johann Ragnarsson/Shutterstock, p46 keith morris/Alamy Stock Photo, p47 irin-k/Shutterstock, p48 SN Thomas Photography/Shutterstock, p49 wellphoto/Shutterstock.

Published by Collins
An imprint of HarperCollins*Publishers*
The News Building, 1 London Bridge Street, London, SE1 9GF, UK

HarperCollins*Publishers*
Macken House, 39/40 Mayor Street Upper, Dublin 1, D01 C9W8, Ireland

Browse the complete Collins catalogue at
collins.co.uk

'Undersea Volcanoes' text © Inbali Iserles 2026. Inbali Iserles asserts her moral right to be identified as the author of this text.
'Investigate Green Power' text © Suzy Senior 2026. Suzy Senior asserts her moral right to be identified as the author of this text.
'The Light Thief' text © Lindsay Galvin 2026
All other text, illustrations and design © HarperCollins*Publishers* Limited 2026

Wandle Learning Trust name and logo © Wandle Learning Trust

10 9 8 7 6 5 4 3 2 1

A catalogue record for this publication is available from the British Library.

ISBN 978-0-00-879097-4

All rights reserved. No part of this publication may be reproduced, stored in a retrieval system, or transmitted in any form by any means, electronic, mechanical, photocopying, recording or otherwise, without the prior written permission of the Publisher or a licence permitting restricted copying in the United Kingdom issued by the Copyright Licensing Agency Ltd, 5th Floor, Shackleton House, 4 Battle Bridge Lane, London SE1 2HX.

Without limiting the exclusive rights of any author, contributor or the publisher of this publication, any unauthorised use of this publication to train generative artificial intelligence (AI) technologies is expressly prohibited. HarperCollins also exercise their rights under Article 4(3) of the Digital Single Market Directive 2019/790 and expressly reserve this publication from the text and data mining exception.

Authors: Lindsay Galvin, Inbali Iserles,
    Samantha Montgomerie and Suzy Senior
Illustrators: Monique Steele (Illo Agency) and
Hannah Drennan (Beehive Illustration)
Publisher: Katie Sergeant
Product manager: Natasha Paul
Education consultant: Charlotte Raby
Project manager: Emily Hooton
Phonics reviewers: Catherine Baker and
    Abbie Rushton
Proofreader and fact checker: Catherine Dakin
Cover designer: Sarah Finan
Cover illustrator: Hannah Drennan
    (Beehive Illustration)
Internal designer: 2Hoots Publishing Services Ltd
Production controller: Sophie Waeland

Developed in collaboration with Wandle Learning Trust

Printed in the UK by Martins the Printers

MIX
Paper | Supporting responsible forestry
FSC
www.fsc.org FSC™ C013254

Made with responsibly sourced paper and vegetable ink

Scan to see how we are reducing our environmental impact.

Collins would like to thank Abi Rothe, Nicola Dickens and the schools involved in the Code pilot for contributing to the development of this book.

Access the planning and resources to teach this book at littlewandlecode.org.uk